Walking Into the Mystery

ISBN: 978-93-90468-68-3

Publishing Year 2020

Published and Printed by:

Sankalp Publication

Head Office: Ring Road 2 Gaurav Path, Bilaspur, Chhattisgarh – 495001

Phones: +91 9111395888 +91 9111396888

Email: support@sankalppublication.com

Website: www.sankalppublication.com

Walking Into the Mystery

Enigma of the Hidden World

Nikhil Sharda

संकल्प

Introduction

If I say there is nothing special in this world, would you believe me?

I know even if you believe me, you will lose faith in me after reading this. But, wait; you will regret it later if you haven't heard the whole truth behind my story. This story is of a boy who lived a simple life like all of us., But one day something mysterious happened that change his life.

It narrates the tale of a boy who had gone on a journey to solve a mystery, only to find something unbelievable

"The story will be narrated in first person."

The story is full of thrills and suspense,–something you would love to read.

Chapter-1
The Story Begins

"Marc, what are you doing?" asked mom in an irritated mood. I didn't know why my mother is always angry and always doubting me.

Perhaps, it was because of my maternal grandfather. I am not saying he was a miser, but he pretended to be like that as same as my mother.

"Marc, you are becoming notorious day by day," she repeated.

Now, my patience was breaking, and I could not wait to give her a reply.

"Mom, what's your problem?" I reverted. She looked at me and ignored. I thought she didn't listen to what I said. Thank God! She didn't hear me.

Suddenly, my dad came inside while all this was happening. I got scared after seeing him not because he came in but I had got my Mathematics exam results that day. However, my dad is a lovely person; on some occasions, he becomes worse than a sea monster.

He has a small mustache with long hairs like a Scottish actor. He is not a miser, but he believes saving money a lot. When it comes to saving money, no one can beat my dad, not even the finance Minister. "He is a gentleman."

"Why does all the misfortune come to me only," my sister said, in a bad mood while she entered the main room. I must agree that she is brilliant in her studies, but is never satisfied with her results.

You must have seen a lot of people like this for sure.

My dad asked her the reason for her sadness; as usual, she said that she got only 98 percent this year. "Literally, everybody in my house was mad," my subconscious mind reverberated. "She got 98 percent, but was not satisfied with it."

The only person who understands me in my home is Kuro. No, he is not a human! He is a dog–a Golden Retriever–and my most loyal friend. If I get a chance to go on a vacation with someone, I will take him only because he doesn't argue. He is neither a blatherskite nor a human; the reason why I like him the most. He has very soft ears like a silk muffler with cushiony fur-like hair on his body. I sometimes rest my neck, making him functions like a pillow for me, and he doesn't utter. He is a friendly dog and loves to make friends; his ears can be compared with those of a rabbit as they can feel any danger coming towards them. Kuro recognizes a person by smelling them and prefer good people as friends. If you want to know more about Kuro, then calling him a dog will not do justice. I always assumed him as a unique dog because his behavior is not similar to any other dog. He is quite an intelligent dog and even knows what is right and what is bad for him. Kuro is so smart that I think if he could speak, then today he would have been a rich.

Let's not talk about being rich. I am so rich, you can't even imagine.

Once upon a time, when I asked my dad for a PlayStation, he bought me a cassette game instead of the Play Station. But still, I was happy because I did not expect even that. But my dad is the dearest to me. It would not be wrong to say that richness is in karma.

I believe I am not as bad as my mother portrayed.

Oh! I forgot to tell you about my dad's occupation. Well, I did not know anything special about his work at that time. It's tough to understand his mind as it is full of extraordinary imagination and thoughts. Whenever I tried to understand his ideas and opinions on living a great life, he confused me more. But, that was not his fault.

"I am a man with extraordinary thinking!" Dad said while he was sitting on the chair outside the Veranda of our house, taking nature's breeze and reading today's newspaper.

"Too old NEWS," dad snarled angrily. It was my dad's nature to find out faults in each and everything, including his own child. It was today's newspaper, but I couldn't say this directly to him because I was not interested in seeing his hand to come behind from the newspaper towards my face at the speed of a falcon. "He is my dad after all," I mulled calmly. One should know two things about my dad, in better words, his two secrets whose truth I didn't know. 1) There was no fixed time for him to come back home from his work. 2) What he actually did?

Whenever my mom asked him about his work, he only said that he worked in a club and at random times given by the club. After all, we were having no problem with dad's odd job because he was earning enough to run the family with ease and was preparing to buy a new house.

"Buying a new house," mom said in an excited mood.

"This was my dream to buy our own house," she said excitedly in a way never before.

I asked my dad about the new house, and he told me that he will be going to buy a new home for our family very soon. Afterwards, our conversation ended, and we got back to our work as everything was normal, without much excitement.

"Yes! My vacations are about to start," I said to myself in a cheerful mood. I said it too loudly that my mom got disturbed and ordered me to go outside and let her do the household works in peace. "Now, I have to go out for some time," I murmured with no energy left inside me. My mom suggested me to go to my friend's house and come back after two hours.

"That's the first time my mom herself suggested to go to my friend's house to play," I said to myself while staring at my mom, working in the kitchen.

I quickly took a piece of bread from the fridge and left for my friend's house. My dog Kuro also came with me. While on the way to one of my friend's home, I saw many new shops. "It's had been too long since I got out of my house," I recalled in my mind. "A lot of new shops have opened in the market." I never got a chance to go out in the market because my mom did all the shopping. She preferred buying everything for me and only took me to buy clothes. That's how much protective my family is. One thing good about my family is we never do complain of each other.

Finally, Kuro and I reached the destination. I rang the bell at Peter's house. "Bell ringing–Bell ringing."

"Peter, see who is on the door," his mom yelled. Her shrill voice reached me from the other side of the door. One should know three things about Peter. 1) His full name was Peter Rhodes. 2) He was a mamma's boy. 3) He was a genius in Science.

Chapter-2
With Friends

I must say that Peter was my best friend because he not only helped me in studies but also understood me very well. He also loved playing with me and doing gossips about our other friends. "That's all we do!"

Our talks were always humorous. Before entering his house, I tied Kuro's leash to his caller and made him sit at the garden's gate. Although I knew that Kuro would not go anywhere, he still had to be tied up because Peter's mother could not bear a dog roaming inside her house. I can understand how it feels to be packed inside one place, but that was only my left choice. I finally stepped my feet inside his room directly from an outdoor gate connected with his room.

"Oh! Such a nice room you have," I said like I was in Heaven.

"My eyes were only on that PlayStation that was kept under the TV. I was so engrossed in it that I could hear Peter's voice too slowly.

"I got my first love," a voice came from my heart.

The look of that Play Station was really cool. I felt like it was calling me.

"Marc, what happened to you?" Peter said in a sudden shock.

"Everything is fine," I exclaimed. But really, that PlayStation had put me in deep thinking.

"Shall we play FIFA on PlayStation?" He asked.

For a second, it felt like he snatched the words away from my mouth.

"Yes, for sure!"

Then we started playing FIFA and many more games. We were really enjoying it.

"I am winning, yeah!" He yelled suddenly, so loudly that my ears started paining.

Everything was going very well. After playing, Peter and I decided to go out and call other friends to play real football. "We were not inspired by FIFA." "Just wait, I am coming in few minutes," Peter said as he was going to Toilet. In that meantime, I was wondering some other games CDs that were lying on the bed. "Fifteen, sixteen, seventeen," I was counting the number of CDs he was having, inside my mind. The collection was impressive, and I knew that I could not afford that much.

"Common, let's go," He called, cheerful after getting light in weight. "Now, we both were ready to go out."

I took Kuro from the garden's gate, where I left him and ran to the house's entrance gate. "It was an exit gate for us." We both eventually left for Ben's house. Ben was also our good friend. He was not good at studies but was excellent in Sports. Ben was a Martial Art champion and liked participating in competitions, especially the sports competitions. Ben’s house was half a mile away from Peter’s home. Peter and I decided to go to Ben's place first and go to another's house afterward. We started walking, but at this time, while walking, even a single step felt like somebody had put a rubber tire on our legs.

“May GOD protects us,” Peter said. “Till now, we had only covered half-distance.”

“It was the day time, and we were full of sweats.”

“If Peter had not been with me at that time, I might not have even thought of going to Ben's house,” I said in my mind only.

We were on a journey and our only destination at that time was to reach Ben’s house.

“How much is left?” Peter asked.

His body was full of sweats. This was only because of the hot sun that was glowing just above our head. Peter and I kept talking on the way; otherwise, it would be difficult for us to even stand in that Sahara Desert. “Assumed the Roads as the Great Sahara desert.”

Chapter-3
That Stranger

Peter and I finally was about to reach Ben's house. Now we were only 50 meters away from his home. Ben's place was in front of us now, and we only had to walk a few steps to get our destination.

"We got the Heaven," Peter said, in a stress-free mood releasing his breath. "That feeling was the same for us as a thirsty got water." We both were happy now, and I was about to ring the bell.

"Oh, no! What we will do now?" he yelled suddenly, staring at me. "Peter suddenly screamed as if the earthquake had occurred."

"What happened to you?" I asked Peter.

"Have you forgotten that we have to go after Ben's house to Emily's house too," He replied with full of stress-filled in him.

"As soon as he said this, I realized that I had forgotten about Emily."

"Oh! Emily," I replied with slight happiness on my face. Emily was neither my best friend nor my girlfriend. I liked Emily but saying this to her directly was not possible for me.

"I believe she also likes me," I thought.

"That was just equal to seeing a big dream."

"Oh Yes, Emily? "We will go to Emily's house, taking Ben with us," I said.

"I am left with no energy and cannot go to Emily's house," Peter replied. "He too was not wrong in his place because I don't even go if I don't like her" "Well, I couldn't tell this to Peter."

"We both were standing outside the Ben's house gate. I was about to move my hand to ring his house bell."

Suddenly, a voice came from our back that sounds similar to the voice of my friend Ben.

"Hey Marc and Peter, How are you?" Ben asked in a gentle voice.

Peter and I realized that this was Ben's voice, we moved our face slowly toward our back from where the voice was coming.

"I saw Ben eating an ice-cream and was coming from somewhere with Emily" I got surprised to see Emily with Ben. Peter was also surprised to see Emily in front of him.

At this point, we both were thinking the same thing. We don't need to go to Emily's house now because Emily was standing exactly in front of us. However, Ben was not going to go anyway.

"Hi, Ben and Emily," we both said together. "After looking at them, it seems like they were waiting for us only to come. "Emily was looking gorgeous as she always looks."

"I am fine," Emily and Ben said together fruitfully. I first looked at Emily and then towards Ben. "They both do not look good together," I told myself, in mind with jealousy. I wanted Emily and

Ben to stand a little bit apart from each other. I was finding some way to execute this, but how?

"Hey guys, now we have all got together, so why not do group study," Emily said. "Let's study together!"

Well, I don't like group study at all, but Emily asked this, that's why I agreed without arguing. She smiled at me because she liked my reply.

"Group Study! Really?" Ben said rudely as he didn't like the idea of group study. "So Boring."

Peter was also not looking very happy with this idea but didn't say anything because Emily might feel bad. I was the only one to accept Emily's suggestion. That doesn't sound good!

"OK, leave it, let's play a game," Emily said as she understood our face. It seemed she know our likings.

"If you say, then we can do group study instead of playing games," Peter said in sarcasm. He said that just for formality but will never stand on it.

"So it is confirm, we will go to the park," Emily said, as she was now fully final with her decision.

"We all agreed."

We decided to go to the park that was just in front of Ben's house as suggested by Emily. "Let's Go!" We yelled, showing our team spirit.

"We had no equipment to play, so we decided to talk with each other." We decided to sit on a bench that was right in front of the park's fountain. Now it was the time of the evening. At this time—I was very delighted because I was sitting next to Emily, and it seems as if my exhaustion was over.

"Then we all started talking with each other—about the school, friends, studies, and a lot more."

Suddenly I saw an uncle standing on the other side of the same park—looked quite gray in appearance. He was distributing free chocolates in the park.

I told my friends to look at him.

"They look at him and ignored."

"Why you ignored him? He is distributing chocolates for free!" I said because I wanted those free chocolates.

"Don't you know that we should not taking anything from a stranger?" Ben muffled, pretending to be an intelligent child.

"I know, but he does not look strange, is he?" I asked.

"He seems very decent—who was happy by distributing candies to the children."

I convinced my friends to get those candies, and they agreed for once.

"After that, we all got up from the bench and started moving toward that uncle distributing chocolates"

"That movement was relatively slow."

"Wait!—I don't eat chocolates so you can take it—I will only come with you," Emily said as she was having fear of something. We all agreed in the best way possible.

We all moved towards the older man and immediately asked him to give us chocolates. I was standing in the middle knowing that I will get the candies first.

"Uncle-uncle-uncle." We yelled.

Till now, he was busy in distributing candies but as soon as he listened our voice and saw us, his senses flown away. He raised his eyebrows with immense shock on his face. I was literally not knowing the reason behind his strange behavior.

"I thought he went on epileptic seizures."

He was still seeing us only. "Oh, I think he was seeing me only."

"What's happening to uncle?" I asked my friends. They were also confused and seems to have no answers for this. That uncle was still staring at me only. He seemed to be scary now.

"Uncle, why you are looking at me only?" I asked with a doubt rising inside my mind. He gave no answers to my question.

"You're the choose one—I found you!" He started saying. "Pointing me like I was their King's son"

Now I was more confused than before. The old man's talks seemed a little strange but did not seem to lie.

"Ben, what are you doing?" Ben's mom asked loudly—standing outside the park. As Ben's house was in front of the park so his mom could easy see everything we all were doing in the park from the balcony of her house.

We all turned our faces and started looking at Ben's mother

"Nothing special mom, we were just taking chocolates," Ben replied his mom.

"From whom?" Ben's mom asked—she was still outside the park.

"Mom, from the uncle," He replied.

"From which uncle?" His mom asked as her mind was full of doubts.

I thought Ben's mother could not see that Uncle from outside.

"Uncle standing behind us," Ben replied.

"There is nobody Ben!" His mom answered in an irritation.

As soon as Ben's mother said this, all of us immediately turned around to see that older man.

"Where did he go?" We started asking from each other doubtfully "Don't lie—it's not good," Ben's mom said.

"No auntie, we are not lying. He was there with us distributing chocolates few minutes ago," we told her.

Then we went outside the park to talk with her.

"Don't lie again and again, STOP IT! I was seeing you all from the balcony from the starting and there was nobody," Ben's Mom replied.

Now we were all completely baffled about what happened to us a few minutes ago. We didn't ask anything more from anyone because we knew that nobody will believe us now.

Peter and Emily thought that they were so lost in the talk that they started seeing an Old Uncle but a deep doubt was there in everybody's mind. We cannot even describe that older man because we had seen him once only and that was also for few minutes.

Ben's mom called Ben and he left. Now, Emily and Peter were left with me. Now we all were getting late for our homes. One by one, everyone left for their house. Nobody had talked about that uncle on the go, everyone seemed to think that it was all our misconception.

"I knew that there was something—it was now a mystery."

Chapter-4
In Night

Now it was going to be night, so Kuro and I left to go back home. All the way through, I kept thinking about that man whom I had seen in the park. I wondered who the man was and where he disappeared. I was only thinking about him and why he said—I am that chosen one.

I reached home — took out the leash of Kuro and entered the house.

"So you have come, firstly go and wash your hands and face," mom said as soon as she saw me entering the house.

"Where were you?" She asked normally.

"I was with friends at Ben's house," I replied. "I moved away."

It was all normal for her, and she did not ask any more questions. I went to the washroom to get fresh. Even in the bathroom, I was thinking about that man as if he sticks in my mind. I was trying to divert my wind but was unable to do so.

I finally came outside of the washroom after washing my face. "I am feeling fresh now," I said to myself. I started moving toward the kitchen to see what my mom had made in the dinner.

I opened the lid of the casserole to see what my mom has made for us. I opened it and saw that there was nothing in it.

"Mom, where is the food?" I shouted. "I was hungry."

"Mom entered the kitchen."

"Oh! Sorry I forgot to tell you that today we are going to have dinner at a restaurant," she said it so happily and loudly that I started jumping.

"Really? It will be fun then," I said. "I got enthusiastic."

After that, I went to my room to get ready, and in a few seconds only I got ready. But my sister was still not prepared. She was doing makeup as if we were going on her wedding. My mom was also waiting for her.

"Hurry up dear, we have to go today only," Mom said in a slight funny mood.

"Mom, have you given the food to Kuro?" I asked

"Yes, you were in the kitchen while I was giving him food," she answered. "Let's Go Now."

I wondered that my sister has come out of the room and is ready to go. We wore our footwear and came out of the house. "I locked the door and put the keys inside my pocket."

My sister and I sat at the back seat of the car and my mom was going to drive the car. She started turning on the car, but the car engine was not starting. Two minutes had passed and the car engine was still not starting. I looked at my sister's face, and by only seeing her face, I understood that she is also thinking the same as what I am thinking.

"Mom, I think the car will not start so it's better eat whatever is available in the house." I said. "My sister showed her support toward me."

"Yes, you are right! Get out the car then," mom said sadly as she was disappointed after not taking us to the restaurant.

After that, we all got out of the car and entered the house.

"Now my appetite had completely gone."

I directly went to my room without talking to anyone. I laid on my bed, and tried to sleep but I was unable to sleep too early.

"Three to four hours had passed."

"While on bed, I felt a little strange and some strong feeling was coming if something bad will be going to happen."

I went downstairs, and saw my mom sitting near the window.

"It was raining outside—Clouds were thundering."

My mom was waiting for my dad to come. She seemed a little tensed than usual.

"Mom, what happen?" I asked her.

"Marc, I am waiting for your dad. He has not come home till now," Mom said.

"She started to cry."

My mom was little possessive towards my dad.At this moment, I did not know what to do and how to behave. The thunderstorms were also scaring my mom.

"Mom don't worry, everything will be fine," tranquilized her. "It didn't not seem to work."

All of a sudden, our house bell rang.

"Who has come at this time," mom asked. "Her mind got diverted."

"Mom, He will be dad for sure!" I smiled.

I immediately ran to open the door.

"I opened the door."

"Nobody is here!" I shouted.

Suddenly my eye fell on the ground. I saw a letter lying over there. I picked up that letter, locked the door, and went to my mom to show her that letter.

"A letter! Which courier service send letters at this time?" she asked as it was 1 in the night. "There was no postman also."

"I don't know mom and there was no postman also at the door," I replied. "Let's open the letter."

I grabbed the letter and opened it. "Oh! I am unable to read this," I said. "It was written in some other language."

"She snatched that letter from my hand." "Oh!—German," she began.

My mother knew German because her mother was from Germany.

She started reading that letter. I was unable to understand because she was pronouncing the words in German only.

As soon as she read some lines of the letter, she quickly started reading the rest of it in speed. It seemed something special was there in that letter.

"All of a sudden my mother went numb." Tears started coming out from her eyes. "The letter came as a complete shock. I had a lot of questions, but I went silent after seeing my mother crying.

"Mom, Calm down," I tranquilized her. "It didn't seem to work."

"Marc, Go to your room!" she said equivocally. "Leave me alone for some time!"

For a while, I went silent. I thought leaving her alone for some time as she will feel good herself after sometime. I went out and sat right behind the wall to the door's right, hearing her crying.

"What could be written in that letter because of which my mother started crying with despair?" I assumed.

I started thinking a lot of things and a lot of bad thoughts started rising inside my mind.

"Enough is enough," I said to myself. "Gathering confidence."

I stood up and went to my mom.

"Mom, Will you tell me what was there in that letter?" I asked her as my mind was full of questions at that time. I was getting confused already.

"Your dad is no longer in this world," she said. "She was dejected."

"What? When and how did this happen?" I asked, in a pain that I was unable to bear."

"I understand what must be going on your heart, but it's true," She replied, "accepting the truth."

I felt everything was over for a moment. I sat on the ground and put my hands over my head — got numb. "It was the worst day of my life."

Chapter-5
Only Mysteries

For the next few days, I tried to forget about the letter, but I could not. I could not stop nagging Mom with a thousand questions. What was actually written in that letter? Why had we not gone to find dad? Why is she believing that my dad is no more? What is she hiding from me? Eventually, my mother put a halt on my interrogation and told me that the subject is now closed and asserted to accept the truth

"Accepting the truth? Don't know what happened to my mother!" I said to myself without releasing the words from my mouth.

I saw that my mother was hiding a lot of things from me. Perhaps, she wanted to keep me away from those secrets.

My sister also had many questions in her mind but did not asked a single question after hearing the news of our dad's death.

"I was pretty much sure that there's some big reason behind my dad's disappearance."

It was very difficult for me to believe that my dad was no more.

After some time, I went to my mother and again asked her to tell me something.

"You are still stuck on the same thing!" she said calmly. "It was just a bad incident that can happen with anybody."

"You are hiding something from me but will not be able to hide for long because I will find the secret," I said. "I moved away."

This time I was in deep thinking and suddenly wondered about that man whom I had met in the park. I was wondering if that man could have some connection.

Thousands of questions were rising in my mind.

I could not forget that man's words "You are the chosen one."

"But what relation could he have with that situation?" I thought.

Suddenly, I wondered about that letter because of which this whole problem had started. I quickly dived outside the room and started searching for the letter. I kept searching for the whole house—bedroom, kitchen, drawers of each room, and everywhere. I tuned everywhere but I didn't see that letter anywhere. Finally, I quit up searching for that letter and came back to my room.

"Where my mom has kept that letter," I said to myself annoyingly. "The letter was the root of the problem."

Suddenly, I realized that I have forgotten to see one place where the letter could definitely be "STOREROOM."

"How can I forget searching in the storeroom," I asked myself, smiling softly.

I quickly stood up and went to the storeroom. The storeroom was at our back of the house, just at the right corner of the old backyard. Our storeroom was neither too big nor too small and was an average size store room. Anybody rarely used to go there because there were a lot of spider webs inside the store room as it was of my grandfather's time.

I opened the door of the store room. "Door produced a crackling sound while opening."

That was the first time I went to the storeroom.

"Too dark it is," I said as I was unable to see anything inside the storeroom. "Full of darkness and spider webs."

I searched if there was any switch of the light or not. I started touching the wall inside of storeroom. "I could feel the cracks of the wall."

Finally, I got a switch on the wall and turned it on. "The bulb was dim, and was producing a lot of heat also."

"I was now able see something due to some light."

I went inside the storeroom a little more. I saw a lot of junk along with big-big old carton boxes. I started searching for that letter.

Firstly, I went to the right of the store room and looked for the letter but nothing was there. Then I started searching for that letter on the right side.

Abruptly, my eyes fell on a dusty carton book that was looking different from others. It was slight golden in color and was made up from a tough substance. “I was unable to guess the substance.”

That box was looking extremely different from all of the boxes.

“I cleaned the dust over the box”
I see that the letter was lying on the top of box. Suddenly I heard my mom’s voice calling me to eat something. I quickly took that letter from the box and ran towards my room.

“Yes Mom, I am coming in 2 minutes,” I shouted from my room.
Maybe she didn't get to know that I was in the store room. It was a good sign for me. I took out that letter and keep it under the drawer so that nobody could find it.

I then went to eat something and came back after eating. After that, I sat on the bed and took out of that letter from the drawer.
I started reading that letter.

“BLA TOHS KURMANA,” I began.

I was unable to understand the words that were written in that letter because it has been written in some other language.

I kept the letter back in the drawer and started thinking of some other solution that could help me. I thought that it will be better for me to give the letter to someone who know German except my mother. If she had even a clue about this whole scandal, it would have become very bad for me.

I didn't know anybody who knew German. I then went to my sister and asked her if she knew anybody who know German.

"No, I don't anyone who knows German," She said.

Suddenly, she replied again saying "There is an Archive on the Stuart Street and an uncle who sit there perhaps know German."

I got really happy after knowing this. This was the first time my sister helped me in something.

"By the way, why are you asking this," she asked doubtfully.

"Nothing, just a little project," I replied her with a fake smile. "I moved away."

"It was going to be night so I decided to go that Archive shop next day."

"I was not worried about the time because my summer had started."

My only aim at that time was to find out the secret of my dad's disappearance.

On the very next day morning—I picked myself up, made myself focused, build my determination and went to the Archive that my sister had told.

"On the way, I faced a lot of problems in searching that Archive but finally found it.

"Now I was one step away to meet the man who could probably tell me something about that letter."

Chapter-6
Finding the Secret

The building was looking quite old and antique. It was totally different from the other buildings in the area as it was made just few years after Queen Victoria demise. After seeing that place, I felt that maybe at this place, I can get to know the answers of my questions.

"Finally!" I shouted. "I was excited."

I opened the entrance door and went inside. I saw the interior of the building. The inside sight was so beautiful that it was impossible to guess its beauty from the outside.

For a while I forgot everything and drowned in seeing the beauty. The walls were having beautiful antique tiles with beautiful carvings done on it. "It was giving completely looking like a attic of a King's palace."

The floors were made using solid and natural woods but with a good groove system as same as in modern floors.

I was seeing each and everything finely. Suddenly a voice came.

"Hey do you have to buy something?" Said the man who was sitting at the reception, in a rough high tone while staring at me"

He was looking quite angry as most of the aged man looks when they cross certain age limit.

"No sir, I haven't come here to buy anything." I said as calmly as I could.

"Then why you have come here if you don't want to purchase anything?" He asked annoyingly.

"At that time, by looking at his face, it seemed that no one had taken even a single book from him in the whole week."

I then told him about the letter that was written in German and asked him if he knew German.

"Oh Yes! I understand German very well." He said as he was confident on his skills.

For a second I felt like I got the man of my dream.

"Can you show me that letter?" He asked.

"Of course!" I handed over the letter to him believing he could read the letter.

He wore his reading glasses and started moving his eyes slowly towards the letter in order to read it.

"OMG! From where you got this letter?" He asked in a surprised manner.

He was stunned to see that letter and started laughing loudly. His rough voice started turning into a normal happy tone.

"Sir, Could you tell me what's there in this letter?" I asked him annoyingly as I don't wanted again to see a person behaving like my mom.

"I will not tell, I will show you," He blurted. "Looking knowing everything."

He held my hand and took me to a big room.

"That room was looking like his personal office, and it was totally surrounded with big-big book shelves."

A big rectangular table in the middle on which a lot of documents and manuscripts were lying.

"WOW! Why you haven't told me about this room" I blurted.

"We just met few minutes ago only." He replied while doing something on the wall.

"He was right."

He started changing the orders of the books on the shelves.

I was confused what he was doing with those books.

"He stopped."

As soon as he completed arranging the books, a shelf started to turn on its own.

"I was shocked to see that shelf itself moving because till now, I had only seen these type of things happening in movies only.

"What you did just right now?" I looked at him with doubtful eyes.

"Come with me," He told me to come behind him.

"Where are you taking me?" I asked him, putting my feet slowly-slowly backward.

He then told me to not worry as it was his own place. He asserted me to assume his as my friend.

I was not scared or worried, but going somewhere with a stranger is also not good.

However, I had come to him, not he.

I started moving behind him, taking each steps very carefully. When I entered the gate, it was complete dark inside. But as soon as he clapped his hand 3 times, suddenly lights started to turn on from the back to front in a line. That was not a square or rectangular room but was a straight lane, going towards a golden gate.

"It was looking a sci-fi movie scene." I pinched my hand to see if it's real or fake.

No one would even have imagined that this much of things could be there inside an Archive. I was getting surprised back to back.

Of Course.

"Why have you taken me here?" I asked him.

Suddenly, He pointed his hand toward that golden gate.

"This is not just a golden gate but is way for us to go into that World," he said, as he wanted to go in that world once.

"You are talking about which world?" I asked him. I felt like that man was crazy.

"AMAZINDAR" A world full of magic and treasure, he said.

"Are you kidding? How can there be any other world other than this world?" I asked doubtfully.

"What do you think that apart from this world, there is no other world?" he said, showing his pride.

I was stunned to know about a world where people were magical. The world that was full of magic would definitely be full of fun.

I then asked him to take me to that World.

"If it was so easy to go into that world, then by now I would have gone thousands of times," He replied. "Never gone to that mysterious World"
"Now, give me that key quickly!" He asked me for a key.

"Which key? I am not having any type of Key," I replied him, saying the truth only.

It seemed to me that he was looking for a key that he thought I would have but in reality I was not having any key at that time.

"You don't have key? Then why had you showed that letter to me?" He asked several questions simultaneously.

"Why are you these questions from me? I just have a letter, not any key," I replied him, asserting him to believe me.

"If you don't know anything about the key then how did you get this letter?" he asked. "He was looking for a key to open the gateway to reach that World."

Then I explained him the entire incident that took place on that night and told him about that letter as well. We then came out of that hidden room and sat in his personal office.
Then I asked him about the letter and what he read in that letter. Afterward, He told me that he is unable to read that letter but knew the letter was from AMAZINDAR, the world of magic.

"How did you get to know that the letter is from that world of magic?" I asked him because I wanted to know the truth.

"There are thousands of world present in the Universe and each of them have their own unique existence," he explained. "Amazindar also have one!"

He seemed to know a lot of things about different Worlds. I asked him about his profession and he told me that he was a Professor of Quantum Physics and used to teach students about it but later on the college management kicked him because they thought he is mad. He used to teach about different Worlds also but that was not in the syllabus of students.

I was very surprised to see him, because even after being fired from college, he never gave up in life and went out for the quest.

He spent my entire twenty years searching for another world and finally found the gate but could not find the key that could open the gate.

"That Golden Gate."

"So how will you find the key now?" I asked him.

"I have to wait because no one knows where the key is," he told me with despair.

I felt very bad for him. He had spent his 20 years in finding the door but couldn't find the key that could open the gate.

"Can we try putting different-different keys?" Perhaps one of them can open the door," I said in a hope.

"Have you gone mad?" He replied. "If we do not open this door at once, we will not be able to open it again.

I got shocked after listening this and apologized to him. I was going to destroy his hard work.

He then told me to go home and asked to not tell anybody about his secret.

"I agreed."

After that, I went home and washed my hands and face as usual. Then I gave voice to my mother but no one in the house responded. I felt there was no one at home but suddenly my sister came and told me to pack my bags.

"Where are we going?" I asked her as she told me to pack my bags.

"We are going to our grandfather's house." she replied and moved away.

This time I was very happy as we were going to my grandfather's house that was in Germany.

Yes, you got it right! "In Germany."

My mom and sister were packing their clothes. My aim was only to find the person who could read that letter. They both were planning their vacations but mine was set.

Then suddenly I thought about that person whom I had met in the Archive, but shortly after that I realized that he is unable to solve his own mystery, what he would do to help me.

"He is an intelligent person but is of no use to me," I mulled.

According to me, he himself was a mystery. He didn't even told me his name. He had found a very big thing but that thing will remain of no use until he finds the key. We both were similar in one thing–He wanted to find the key that could open the gate and I wanted to find someone who could read that letter of secrets.

"My next destination was Germany."

Chapter-7
On A Vacation

My mom had already booked the tickets for Germany, and we were about to leave. Then, we left for the airport. We reached the airport and done all the formalities and then sat inside the plane. I was sitting on the seat near the window. My mom and sister were sitting in the third row.

"Why did they give me a seat that was far from both of them," I murmured as they had done injustice to me.

I put my seat belt as the plane was about to take off. After few minutes, the plane was finally in the air above the clouds. I was delighted at that time.
I was seeing the outer view from the window. Getting a window seat was a plus point for me because I could see the outside view of the plane from the window.

My sister and mom were talking with each other but I was confused what I should do. I was in confusion as I didn't know what to do.

I then started talking to a woman who was sitting next to me.

"Hi! How are you?" I began.

"FINE," she said in arrogance.

She was looking very sincere from the face but had no manners in real. She seemed ill-mannered when she replied me in arrogance.

"Why did I talk to her at all?" I regretted.

It was all my mistake to talk with that stranger but all of the strangers are not bad. There was still a lot of time left for the aircraft to reach Germany. I started thinking of doing something else.

Suddenly an air hostess came and asked what I want to eat. I was impressed by her behavior. Her voice was as sweet as a cuckoo. I started comparing that women sitting next to me with the air hostess. No comparison could be made. There was a difference of ground and sky.

"I want pasta to be served on my table," I told the air hostess.

"Of course sir," she replied and went to get my order.

It was a ten hour flight and the time was moving very slowly. Only four hours had been passed. There were still six hours left. I just wanted to relax but my thoughts were stopping me to do so. After some time, I put my feet up and sat in a relaxed position. Then, I started recalling all the mysterious activities happened with me one by one. I started thinking from the very beginning.

"Firstly that old man in the park, later my dad's disappearance, then that secret letter, and then that man at Archive."

"All of these had occurred so quickly that I didn't even get the time to think," I sighed.

I had a lot of questions at that time like–why this all is happening with me only?
Till now, I had not found the person who could me the answer of all of this questions. I didn't lose hope and was still on the journey.

The plane was about to land as we had reached Germany. It was morning time. I hadn't slept in plane even for a minute. My curiosity and certitude did let me sleep. Then, the plane landed and everybody started to come out of the plane. We also came outside the plane and went towards the exit Gate after taking our luggage and completing the check out.

Suddenly I saw my Grandpa standing outside.
"Mom, see grandpa is there," I said to mom. "Pointing my hands towards Grandpa."
"Yes, let's go to that side," she said.

I took the luggage bag from my mom's hand and started to move.

"Grandpa–Grandpa" I started yelling, as fast my steps were progressing towards him.
"Hey my grandson, How are you?" He asked, waving his hands on my head.
"So far it was fine, but now it's awesome," I replied delightedly.

My mom and sister also came after me. Mom touched Grandpa's feet, giving him respect. My Grandpa showed his love towards my sister also.
"Welcome to Germany," he greeted.
My Grandpa is a very loving person and always keeps smiling.

He then took us from the airport to his house in his car. On the way, he was keep talking about his own country. He also told us about the different–different monuments and structures. He promised to show us the entire city of Berlin.

"It's the capital of Germany."

"We reached home and were very excited for seeing Grandma.

This time, my mom entered first and grandma welcomed her.

"Grandma–Grandma," my sister and I started yelling, as fast our steps were progressing towards her." She then waved her hands on our head and gave us blessing.

After some time, all the formalities got ever. We were give separate rooms as they were having no problems on rooms. My grandfather and grandmother lived alone in a very large house. My grandfather was a retired army officer and my grandmother was a retired teacher. They both were living very happily.

Then, we all went into our rooms to get fresh, and came back at the time of lunch. My grandma had prepared my favorite food items.

I like my Grandma because she is the one who understands me and also scold me whenever I do wrong. Everyone should have a Grandmother like mine.

"Let's start the lunch," she said to all of us.

"Of Course!"

She then served us the food and we started eating it.

"Too Yum!" We all said together.

While having the lunch, my grandpa and grandma were talking with my mom. They had asked my mom about her future but she didn't answered. Maybe we were sitting there so she didn't say anything. But, the question they asked was point to be noted.

"Children eat all the food, then after that we will all go to see the Victoria column," my grandpa said excitedly.

He had planned to take us to the Victoria Memorial. My Grandpa is an open hearted person but this time I didn't want to go because if I will go then who will solve the mystery?

"No Grandpa, I will not come," I told him and made an excuse to rest at home.

"He agreed."

After some time, my sister and mom left out for Victoria Column with Grandpa. Grandma and I said bye to them.

"Bye."

After they left, I had enough time to find a person who could read that letter and explain it.

"That letter had become a secret-cum-mystery."

Chapter-7
Quest for the Right Person

"Marc, what are you doing outside?" my grandma gasped. "They have gone."

I listened to my Grandma and came inside. Now I had a lot of time as my mom had gone with my Grandpa and my sister and will not be going to come before night. It was a great chance for me to ask my Grandma about my dad. This was the first time when I was feeling good on my mom's absence.

I came inside the house and went to my own room first. I opened my luggage bag and took out the letter which I received the night when my dad went missing.

"Whenever I remember that night, don't know why I get sad," I looked at the sky from my window.

I sat on my bed holding that letter in my hand, and started weeping because my father's absence was pricking me like a needle. I started thinking of myself as a failed son as I was proving to be incapable to discover the secret behind the sudden disappearance of my father. All the doors seemed to be closed for me, I sighed with tears.

"Whenever you feel that all the doors are closed, then think about your destination as far as you had decided to go." My grandma said suddenly while entering inside my room, as she saw my weeping.

"You don't know anything Grandma, Please leave me alone," I said to her annoyingly.

"Okay, but I thought you were looking for your dad," she said.

As soon as she said this, I stood up from the bed in a jolt. I was stunned to hear what she said.

"Grandma, how do you know that?" I asked her quickly without thinking of further. She seemed to know something.

"No sorry, just a little while ago, you said that I don't know anything and were asking me to leave too," she replied as she felt bad after my rude behavior.

I felt very bad for my behavior but my intention was not to hurt my Grandma at all. That was just a stance of time.

Of Course

"Sorry Grandma, I should not have treated you like that," I apologized my Grandma for my rude behavior. I never wanted to hurt anybody.

"You realize your mistake, that's all for me," She replied with a smile on her face. She then waved her hands on my head and fondled it. She had forgiven me and was no more upset from me.

After that I immediately looked at my grandmother and asked how she knew I am finding the secret of my dad's sudden disappearance.

"He was my son before being your father," grandma said proudly, looking into my eyes.

My Grandma was a very brave woman. She did not panic even after knowing about my father's disappearance. Her each and every words at that time were valuable for me because I had completely lost the hope to find my dad. My head was down and I was upset at that time.

"What are you holding in your hands? Show me," she grabbed the letter from my hand and started seeing it.

Suddenly, she became numb after reading that letter. That letter gave her a shock and she was totally in silence after reading the letter. She was seeing the letter like if my dad was there in it.

"I am unable to understand why the people who see this letter are going in shock," I imagined. Firstly my mom, afterwards that man in the Archive, and now my Grandma.

"A lot of people are seeing the letter but nobody is knowing what is written in it," I realized. Everyone who read the letter had some excuses. My last hope left was with my Grandma. Now my grandmother was my last hope who could tell me something as she knew German language very well.

"Grandma, do you know anything about this letter?" I asked her, with hope.

"This letter is from another world," She replied. Her widened eyes and gaping mouth were clearly indicating the presence of fear and surprise in her after reading that mysterious letter.

I was very surprised to hear the words my grandmother said because she told me the same thing that the man in the Archive told me. Both of them had talked about the hidden world of magic.

"Are you talking about Amazidndar? the world of magic?" I asked and it seemed that she knew the origin of that letter.

"How do you know about Amazindar?" She asked me surprisingly, and was looking into my eyes as if I had done a murder.

She then started asking me a lot of questions simultaneously without even giving me the time to speak. Her forehead was sweating profusely and she began to come in tension.

"The person who told me about this letter was a former professor of Quantum Physics," I replied.

For while, I forgot all my questions and began giving answers of her questions. She was asking questions back to back.

"Now stop! I came Germany to ask you about Dad and you started asking from me only," I looked at her with disappointment and then went to the garden as she seemed to be incapable of giving me the answers at that moment.

I sat on the garden's chair and started looking at the sky, seeing its limit. I had not loosen hope till now because somehow, my Grandma had also given me motivation indirectly. Suddenly someone fondled my head behind me, I looked back with a jerk. That was my Grandma!

"Come with me, I will show something you are looking for," My grandma said with no expression on her face but it seemed to be a sign of seriousness.

Then I went with her at her behest. She took me to a small room full of dirt and junk. It seemed like nobody has cleaned the room from a very long time. She started cleaning the photo frames on the walls.

"Why you took me here grandma?" I asked her. "All these photo frames you are seeing hanging on wall are the certificates and degree achieved by your dad. He was an excellent student of Quantum Physics," Grandma told me a lot about my dad that I didn't know.

"Student of Quantum Physics!"

"If he was such a good student, then why did he work at a club," I asked my Grandma instantaneously after her reply. Even our dad never told us anything about it. Why a student of Quantum Physics will work at a Club?

"Have you ever seen your dead working at club from your eyes?" She asked me as if she was knowing all the truth but was hesitating in telling me. Her question suddenly put me in a thinking. She made me think.

"Yes, you are right! I have never seen my dad going or coming from a club," I replied, thinking about her job again. Dad just had told me that without any proofs. I started feeling a little more complex as new-new secrets were coming out simultaneously.

"What do you want say grandma? Speak straight away," I told her to say everything clearly without making the rings of things.

This all was attracting me toward knowing the truth but at the same time, a lot of questions were there in my mind. My Grandma started telling me more about my dad.

"Your dad was a great student of Quantum Physics and wanted to spend his entire life in studying and knowing about different Worlds and dimension," She said, showing intense keenness of my dad towards knowing different worlds.

"Did he discover any world after that?" I asked, with keenness of knowing more about my dad because not even my mom could know this much about my dad. I looked toward my grandma.

"Yes, He found that World," My grandma replied with her eyes up, remembering everything about my dad.

I was completely astounded after hearing that. I assumed my dad as a secret himself. My dad was mysterious person but he will be this much mysterious, I didn't know. And after all, it was a heart wrenching secret.

"Really! Then where is that world? How can we go there?" I started asking all of these questions from my grandma as I got more interested in knowing the truth and his discovery of a New world.

"Wait! Don't take this much of interest in this because I don't want you to repeat what your father did," She looked at me fearfully. "No, Never," she mumbled with fear as if she knew the bad consequences of the work, she was hiding something from me at that time.

"I don't even know what my dad had done and it's my right to know everything about dad," I said to her, with a positive attitude.

"By now, I came to know that my father had a lot of secrets, but now the time has come to remove the curtain from all those secrets," I contemplated my thoughts and that all seemed totally true. A huge conversation was going between me and my grandma.

"I can't tell you more than that because maybe you can get stuck in that swamp too," she said worryingly, looking at me.

"All these things are being repeated back, but this time I will not let this happen," she mumbled with fear, looking tensed as her forehead was sweaty.

She got so much tensed that I decided not to ask any more questions from her at that moment and requested her to take rest. I asked her to go and rest in her room I can ask her questions later.

I then went with my grandmother till her room. I had stopped asking her questions for a while and then came back to my room with that letter in my hands.

"It is not right to question her so much. And anyway, now that age is cursed. When she will feel a little better, I will ask her everything," I contemplated all the probabilities inside my mind.

"That secret would have been exposed if my grandmother would have told me everything, but alas she did not reveal anything at that time."

I then laid down on my bed with a jerk, wondering what my grandmother was hiding about my dad.

I put my hands under my head and face towards the ceiling of the room. At that time, I was only thinking about my dad and grandma.

I was surprised to hear from my grandma that the world, whose name was 'Amazindar', was discovered by my dad. It was a heart wrenching secret because my dad had told everybody that he just used to work at a club. I started assuming all the possibilities that could be there in the mystery.

"It means that my father was the creator of the key that can open the gate of Amazindar which also signifies that my dad had gone to that World," I surmised with an astounded reflection of expression on my face.

It was difficult to believe, but the truth had been revealed by my grandma herself. That man whom I had met in the Archive was absolutely correct about the existence of the world of magic and I thought he is mad. "The World really exist."

"I want to see that World, at least once!"

I expressed my wish. Maybe, my dad could be there, and perhaps I could bring my dad back.

"My Grandma was the only person who could tell me the way to go into that World."

Chapter-9
Moving Forward

It was soon going to be night. My grandpa along with my mom and sister were about to come. I was in my room and was thinking the way to find something more about my dad and his discovery of the Amazindar.

"My dad was hiding such a big secret from me and I did not even get a hum of it," I said to myself as the truth was so big that it could change the entire technology of the world and could bring a massive development.

My dad did what the great people of the world are also unable do till now. He must have been a great student of Quantum Physics as this thing can also be expected from a Physics student only.

I was extremely stunned and wanted to tell this secret to everybody I know, but then I realized that there are a lot of people in this world who will try to use that World for their own sake and will destruct it entirely.

"But no one knows where's the key that can open the gate of Amazindar, the world of magic," I sighed, with disappointment.

Although, I was the son of the person who had found the gateway to that world but I myself got to know a few moments ago.

It was a shocking secret for me but I hadn't taken a lot of time to accept and admire the truth. I hadn't taken a lot of time to believe my grandma, as my grandma never tells a lie. She can die but will never tell a lie.

All the truths were coming out one by one.

"It can't be a coincidence to have all those mysterious people and things in my life," Firstly than man in the park, then the man in the Archive, and afterwards the letter from another World.

"I didn't seem to be a coincidence," I thought. I was on my bed and was pondering all of these things in chronology as per the occurrence.

Suddenly, someone started knocking the door

"Marc, Open the door!"

Oh, she is my mom!

I quickly stood up from the bed and went toward the door. I opened the door and saw my mom standing.

I got worried after seeing my mom as I was thinking perhaps my grandma had told everything to my mom. My heart started beating rapidly. I then looked at her.

"Marc, why you were not listening? I was shouting from the hall but you didn't answer. Now come and have dinner," she said annoyingly as she thought I was not responding her.

"I didn't even realize when she came from outside," I mumbled.

For some time I felt as if my grandmother had told my mother everything but nothing like that was there. My mom was normal and was looking quite well. However, after my dad's disappearance, my mother didn't like to talk much with anybody.

I then went with my mom to have dinner and sat on the dining chair. Everybody was there except my grandma.

I then looked around to see where my grandma is but I couldn't see her around me.

"Where's grandma?" I asked my mom, as grandma didn't seem to be around.

"She is in the kitchen and is preparing food for us," mom replied.

I got shocked after hearing this because she was in her room till sometime back and is making food now. I think she didn't want my mom to know about what happened between me and her. It was a good news because if my mother got to know what had happened between grandma and me, then she would get tensed up and would have stopped me from doing anything. But for god sake, no such thing happened.

Suddenly my grandma came out from the kitchen, holding the casserole in her hands. My mom also stoop up to help her and they brought the vessels from the kitchen together. After bring the food, they both also sat with us.

My sister and grandpa were looking very hungry as they hadn't eaten anything since the afternoon. They just had some chips during the visit at Victoria Column and some other common monuments in Berlin. We started our dinner after praying. It was awesome.

Suddenly, I looked toward my grandma while eating. She seemed normal and was quietly having the dinner. It seemed like she is thinking something. I kept looking for some minutes but she didn't give a look back. It was disappointing.

"Maybe she is not talking to me but why?" I imagined.

It seemed like if she was ignoring me but I had not done anything wrong. My grandpa and sister were talking about the fun they had in seeing the monuments and other places. During the whole meal, both of them kept talking about their day and I kept listening to them. My mom was just saying 'wow–wow' after each sentence of my sister.

My grandma was not giving any reaction to anybody and I knew the reason behind her silence.

"She is hiding something from me and don't want to tell me," I assumed, looking serious. "The way to Amazindar."

I then finished my meal and went to wash my hands. It was a fussy day. I was very tired, and therefore decided to talk with grandma the next day.

"She will also be tired," I assumed.

There were a lot of questions in my mind at that time but asking all of those from her at the moment will not be good because everybody was at home that time.

I then went to my mom.

She was stitching her clothed using the sewing machine.

"Mom, I am going for sleep now," I told her as I didn't want disturbance while sleeping.

She was busy in her own work. She moved her head and up and down and it seemed that she is saying yes.

Then I moved towards my room and locked the door from inside. I was very angry at that time because of my Grandma's behavior.

"If she does not want to talk to me then why should I also?" I self-proclaimed, as it was all going over the head. I had only tried to know about my father from her, but after that conversation, she did not even look at me. I was frustrated.

Suddenly, someone started knocking my door. I told my mom not to disturb me but still. I opened the door and saw my Grandma standing in front of the door. I was stunned and went numb after seeing her. I thought my mom will be there but my grandma was there.

She then quickly came inside my room and asked me to lock the door. She seemed little bit scared. Her face was as if she had done a robbery somewhere and afterwards coming to me.

"Grandma, why have you come here this time and that too like thieves?" I asked her in a very low pitch of voice. "Definitely something is wrong."

I looked towards her face.

"This time is not for all these waste talks, I have come to show you something," She said, in a way she had never talked before.

She made me sit on the bed and went out of the room. Suddenly after few seconds, she came to my room again and this time, she was holding a wooden box in her hands. The box was looking quite old.

"Be seated on your place and don't stand up until I tell you to do so," she said quickly and was very serious.

"I felt certain that she is going to tell me what she was hiding from me."

"The next words will be her and I will be the hearer."

Chapter-10
The Key

"Now whatever I am going to show you, after that you will not ask me any question. If you promise, only then I will move forward," she said to me and asked if I agree with this or not.

I was having no other options then to agree. I agreed with her and asked to show me the thing.

"Okay, now see what I am going to show you." She replied.

She started opening the box which was there in her hands. That moment was relatively slow and was like a suspense scene of a movie. Her hands were opening the box slowly-slowly. Finally, she removed the lid of the box.

The item inside the box was covered with a dark colored cloth. I told grandma to remove that cloth quickly as I was getting impatient to see what's inside it.

She then quickly removed that cloth in a stroke. She looked at me and asked to take out that thing from the box. I was shivering with curiosity.

I slowly moved my hand toward that box and put my hands inside the box to take the thing out. I was doing the same my grandmother was saying.

Suddenly, a violent vibration occurred inside that box and my hand got stuck inside.

"Grandma, what's happening? Help me!"

My hand got trapped into that box and I was not coming out of it.

"Grandma, Help me! Something is there in the box," I yelled for help quickly carefully. "The box started vibrating in a more speed."

I didn't know what is happening. I kept asking my grandma for help.

Suddenly, a blue light came from inside the box and pulled my entire body inside the box with an extreme force. Everything was happening in such a hurry that I didn't even get a second to handle myself.

"When the box pulled my hands inside, I saw only a blue light around me and then I got fainted."

Chapter-11
Entry Into the World of Magic

After some time, I recovered consciousness and found myself in a secluded cave. I stood up and started looking around but nobody was around me and I was there in the secluded cave alone. The cave was neither too dark nor too bright. Partial light was coming from outside.

I then moved towards the point from where the partial light was coming. As near as I went towards that point, I heard the sound of waterfall. The sound was very slow but when I moved more near towards the point, I found that I am behind that waterfall. The cave was hidden behind the waterfall and I am in the cave at that moment.

"What is happening with me?" I confounded as if my body was not feeling well. I was not feeling well and I felt lighter in weight.

Each and everything happening was difficult for me to understand.

"How and when I came here? Where am I?" I imagined, as I didn't know how I came here. I only remembered that I was with my grandma in my room and I had put my hands inside a box and then suddenly a blue light had come from inside the box that took me here.

"Perhaps, I am in Amazindar!" I self-proclaimed because the box that took me here was given my Grandma. She showed me the way to this World.

"I misunderstood my grandmother, but my grandmother helped me to find this world," I realized and felt sorry. "Thanks to grandma who showed me the way.

I then looked around to see if there's any way to go outside that cave. My eyes then fell on the side of the waterfall. There was a small gap there but was enough wide for a person to pass from that gap.

I then moved towards that gap. It was slippery, so I kept on looking my steps carefully while walking. Finally I succeed in coming out of that cave, I sighed with relief.

I then moved my head up.

"WOW! Is it really Amazindar? It's next to Heaven!" I said surprisingly after seeing the look of the World.

When I was in the cave, I didn't even think that this world would be so amazing. It's difficult to express the beauty of that World.

I saw vehicles that were looking like car flying in the air and a person looking like us were driving it. Huge buildings were there but those building were looking extremely modified as I had never seen any structure like that before. The people there were like us only, but their clothes were quite different. They had worn a suit that was looking very distinctive, as those suits were not tie and blazer. They were totally different. It seemed if they were made up of some other type of element which I had never seen before. Most of the people were travelling through air rather than roads. It was totally opposite from our World.

I looked all around me and everyone looked very happy. I was still in little doubt and wanted to get it solved. I wanted to confirm from someone if I am in Amazindar or not. After coming from the cave, I moved towards the road and knocked the door of a random person as I wanted to confirm this from someone.

“Sir, could you tell me where I am?” I asked him very politely.

He started saying something to me but I was unable to understand his words. We both were unable to understand each other because of language dissimilarity.

I then said sorry for disturbing him and then moved forward. I then kept moving forward and had come in a market of items where different type of items were being sold.

I was shocked to see those people in the market because they were using magic to sell their items. They were floating their items into the air and were showcasing their product using magic.

“It’s unbelievable! How they are doing it?” I said surprisingly after seeing their skills and powers.

Each of them were having distinctive magic powers which they were using for earning money. The routine of all of these people were same as of our Earth but their way and the whole framework as well as technology was totally different. It seemed that they are 100 times ahead from us as compared with their world and our world.

That was unbelievable as well as astounding. Amazindar would be a quintessential for a well-developed and modified city.

I was standing on the side of left side of the road and was seeing all of those people. From their cloth to their lifestyle, everything was unique and magical.

Suddenly, my eyes went on each and everybody hands. At the same time I saw that every person who was performing magic had a ring in their hands.

I them moved more closely towards them to see those rings in their fingers, as my curiosity was pulling me towards them to find out more.

"Each ring was having a certain distinctive structure," I noticed. Some of them were having the snake structure on it, some were having tiger and some were having cheetah and a lot more.

"Maybe they are able to perform that magic because of that ring," I assumed as each of their magical powers were different from person to person. Some were stronger and some were less and the only thing that was determining their abilities was a ring. I noticed each of the activity very carefully. They all seemed to be amazing and powerful.

"The world is really amazing," I said to myself as everybody seemed to be amazing there.

There were still some people who were having nothing in their fingers and were not able to perform any magic and therefore could not be as powerful as those people who had rings of powers. People of this world looked exactly like the people of our world, but here every person was recognized by their strength that was in their rings. The ring was making them powerful but they had control those powers and only some selective people were able to do so.

I was standing on the left end side of the market and was observing their activities and their behavior. One thing I got to know at that time was about their language. They were talking in some other language instead of English, I noticed. Suddenly a fellow came and he pulled my hand and snatched me back in a jolt. My hand got hurt.

"Hey! What are you doing?" I asked him angrily as he had pulled my hand in a jolt.

"You are a human being and what are you doing here?" He looked at me and asked surprisingly. He was checking up my whole body and was staring me.

Suddenly I realized how he spoke in English. I immediately raised my head in shock and looked at him.

"How do you know English?" I asked him doubtfully but he didn't answer.

It was quite shocking to see a man who knew English here as every person I saw in Amazindar was talking in some other language that I didn't understand.

"Just tell me how you came here," He asked again and had ignored the questions I asked from him.

"Just mind your own business and why I will tell you!" I replied in attitude, being slight aggressive.

He was asking a lot of questions but I didn't felt any need of telling him the reason.

"I don't mean anything to you, but maybe you don't know that humans are not allowed to come in our World and even if a human comes, then their punishment is very dangerous," He replied looking towards me, putted his eyebrows up.

I got tensed after hearing that as I am also a human and I didn't knew the punishment given by them to a person who come in their world without permission.

"Now what will happen?" I looked at him in stress and asked him quickly.

He then replied and said that I will be hanged by them if they will get to know about me.

"They will just move their magic ring and immediately you will die after that," he said, in a way as he don't have the feeling of humanity for anyone.

"Of Course, They were not humans!"

"Our king is a very powerful person and will not tolerate the entry of a human in his World," He continued telling me about their law.

That Stranger words were bothering me more than him because he was only talking about my death. I then told him to leave me as I will manage on my own.

He asked me to come him with him as I will get caught if I will roam here and there on the roads like this. My appearance and behavior were not like those people and were like humans, Of Course.

"Maybe you are right but don't take is as favor because I will play you for this soon," I told him vigilantly as I didn't want a favor of anyone.

In my mind, I knew that I am taking his help but I didn't want to tell this to him, as maybe he could think that he had done a favor on me. I didn't want these problems to happen.

He then gave me a big white color scarf and told me to cover my face and come behind him. I then started following him and finally reached his home where he used to live. It was a very small house and was not connected with any other house as it was not a permanent house and was just a temporary house.

"I built this house for myself as I don't have any family," he said to me normally while walking slowly.

I felt very bad for him because I could understand his pain as I was also going through that same pain at that time.

He then took me inside his house and told me to sit for few minutes. He went to kitchen to see if something was there in the kitchen or not. After some time, he came to me and given me a cup of a drink that was golden in color.

"What's this?" I asked quickly as the drink seemed to be quite different. I had never any drink of this color and fragrance before. The drink was shining and bubbling. It seemed hot but when I touched it, it was cold.

"Don't worry, this is just a glass of water of our World," he replied, letting me cool down.

I then took a sip of that drink. As soon as the drink touched my tongue, I started feeling good as that drink was not only tasty but was also magical. The fragrance and color was absolutely magical.

"It's not only tasty but also finished my thirst," I chuckled after drinking the whole drink after taking a sip of it.

"Yes my friend, this is Amazindar's water," He replied in a gentle manner.

"We just met and you assumed me as your friend," I corrected.

He then took those cups and taken them to the kitchen. I was sitting in the hall and looking around to see his house properly. There was almost no difference in his house and Earth's houses but most of the houses here were amazing and magical as well. Each and everything was working automatically but his behavior and lifestyle was exactly similar to those of humans on Earth.

“How he knows English and how did he know I am from Earth,” I suddenly realized as it could not be a co-incident.

Everything was going very well and I hadn’t faced any problem in Amazindar till now. I was having a lot of confusions and was not knowing what to do next. “I had many questions that I wanted to ask him.”

Chapter-12
A Sudden Conversation

It was boring to keep sitting on a chair when you are in a new world, full of mysteries. Not everybody get a chance to go and see a new world. I didn't even know anything much about this world.

"How I will live here," I said to myself, as I had never experienced anything like this before. I need to find my dad as soon as possible.

Suddenly, that boy come back from the kitchen and sat just in front of me, on the opposite side of the table. He kept staring me like I was a monster.

"How did you find the World?" he asked doubtfully.

"It's a very long story, I will tell you later," I replied to him as the anecdote was too long. At that time, I was confused and didn't know where I should go. I was with that boy whose was looking almost similar as my age.

"What's your name?" I asked him.

"My name is Robert but people here call me Rob," He replied, looking at me and smiling.

He was eating something like a wild animal. He didn't seem to be a bad person but was having no etiquettes of eating.

"Really!"

"What's your name?" he gurgled with mouth full of food.

"Yuck!"

"My name is Marc, Marc Faladian," I replied, in a simple manner while looking toward his face that was full of food.

Suddenly he dropped his filled spoon before putting it in his mouth and stood up immediately. He made his eyes dilated and the speed of chewing the food got slowed. He started chewing the food relatively slow.

"I got confused on hid behavior and why he is behaving like that."

He then went to the washroom for a second and came back after splitting the food that was there in his mouth. That moment was not only slow but also silent. A pin drop silence got there suddenly. Everything was well until some time ago and now he started behaving like this.

Suddenly he came to me and stood just two foot away from me. He looked at me.

"HAAHAA—HAHAHAH," he suddenly yelled so loudly that my ears started to pain by his voice.

I quickly took the cloth lying on the table and put inside his mouth with force in order to stop him. He then stopped yelling as I had put a piece of cloth inside his mouth.

"What happened to you? Why are you behaving like this?" I asked him. "His sudden behavior really seemed weird!"

"Are you really Marc Faladian?" he asked surprisingly. "Son of James Faladian?"

"Yes, I am but how do you know my father?" I asked perplexed.

At first, I was astonished after hearing about my dad from Robert but then I realized maybe he knows my dad because he was the creator of the world where he lives.

"I got you!" he said to himself surprisingly. "You're the chosen one!"

His words suddenly made remembered that man whom I had met in the park when I was in my own World with my friends. He was also saying the same thing that Robert said to me. I recalled all of the things at that time.

"Definitely some connection is there between that man and this world," I assumed the possibilities. "I want to know more."

Everything seemed to go as strange as I never expected.

A lot of mysteries, puzzles, secrets, imaginations altogether couldn't even make an interesting movie like my father had made such a beautiful world but had kept this world a secret to me. At that time, I didn't know why but will soon get to know.

I then asked Robert the same thing that I asked from the man whom I had met in the park. That older man didn't answer my question but Robert did.

"Come with me! You will get to know everything," he replied, looking into my eyes with hope. "I know you are having a lot of questions and confusions."

I agreed and followed him without any interrogation as I didn't want to lose this chance to know more about the secret behind my dad's sudden disappearance.

I then followed him wherever he was taking me to because I had started trusting him little bit.

I then followed him wherever he was taking me to because I had started trusting him little bit.

We were going very quietly without letting other people see us. He then took me somewhere and asked me to come inside the house. That house was looking quite old and seemed to be a workshop. We both then entered the house. He took me to the main hall and told me to sit on the floor carpet. It didn't seem to be a simple workshop from inside because everything kept there was moving on its own and all the work was going on by itself without the help of anyone.

Tea kettle was making tea on its own and was making two cups of tea. The broom was cleaning the floor itself and all other normal household works were being done by the instruments only. That all seemed to be horrible. I got scared after seeing that all.

"How all of these inanimate objects moving on its own?" I asked Robert surprisingly, while sitting in hero pose.

"Oh all these—don't worry!" He told me to calm down. "Don't you trust me?"

"I don't. I mean I do, but I don't," I vacillated.

Suddenly, sound of the footsteps of a fellow came and he was coming towards us only.

I got curious to see that person for whom Robert took me here.

Chapter-13
The History

The sound of the feet started intensifying. That man was coming towards us. I was able to hear the sound of his foots clearly.

He then entered the room but he had hidden his face and therefore, I was unable to see his face at that moment. He then came to us and sat on the floor mat that was just five to six feet away from us. Robert also sat on the ground and told me to succumb my head in order to show respect to that man. I did the same as he told me, and then moved my head up.

As soon as I moved my head up, I looked toward that man again and got stunned after seeing his face. He was the same man I had seen in the park when I was in my world instead of this. That man in front of me had given shock to me.

"How you came here?" I asked him surprisingly, as it was beyond expectations. "How is this possible?"

"Just have a glass of water," He replied, smiling at me as if he knew everything.

He was behaving normal but that was not normal for me at that time. Robert had already told him about my identity and origin. When I had met him in the park, he suddenly had disappeared without saying anything and now I met him again here but this time he didn't ignore.

There were so many questions in my mind that I was confused about what to ask first. For every human being, it can be a shocking anecdote that will meet the person he once saw and that too suddenly vanished. The same situation was of mine at that time. I myself didn't know what was happening with me. I was meeting new people one after the other, who were very mysterious also.

I then drank a glass of water that actually was a glass of golden drink which they considered as their world's water. After that, I started asking a lot from question from that man.

"What are you doing here? Where you got disappeared when I had met you for the first time? If you are from this world then what were you doing in my world?" I asked multiple questions nonstop as a lot of confusions were there in my mind that forced me to ask altogether. "Give me the reply."

"Wait, you are going too fast," he huffed, telling to go slowly. "I will tell you everything but this is not the correct time."

"First you should change your clothes because if someone sees you in these clothes then it will go awry," he said. "I am giving you clothes of your size."

I then changed my clothes and wore the clothes that they used to wear. In the beginning, the clothes looked very tight but then in a while, everything started to look good and I felt good.

"Now, you are all ready to listen me," he tempted. "Now hold your back and only listen to whatever I will say."

Robert was sitting beside me and we both sat straight in a comfortable manner and agreed not to interrogate when he will be speaking.

My curiosity level was at the peak as I wanted to know everything, means everything. I wanted to know about this world and truth behind my dad's sudden disappearance.

I had no selfish interest in whatever I wanted to know.

He then started telling me everything from the beginning so that my all confusion could get their answers in the narrative.

He started

"Amazindar was created seven hundred years ago. This world was created seven hundred years ago by a sorceress named Marina. She was the most powerful sorceress of the entire Universe. She named this world as Amazindar. She was a sorceress but was a good and kind queen. She created the people of Amazindar and slowly started bringing many changes in this world. She used to give help and food to her people. She also had an adopted son named Joseph. Joseph was not at all kind toward the people of his kingdom, but Marina never realized this. This world was not magical at that time. It was just like the ordinary world and there were ordinary people who had nothing to do with magic. Many years had passed and Marina was ageing. Despite being a great sorceress, she could not become immortal nor did she wish of becoming. She was worried only about her people and their safety. She wondered what would happen to her people after her death, and no other sorceress would attack this world after she left. She loved her son very much but due to her not being a real son, Joseph did not have the same strength as Marina. All the people knew that Joseph would never become a good and true king, but Marina could not hear anything bad about her son, so we never dared to speak this to Marina. This went on for some years, but one day came when Marina's health deteriorated. The whole people of Amazindar stood outside her palace. Marina's condition was getting worse. Marina also knew that she was going to die very soon, so she made a big decision. She gathered all her strength and made thousands of magical rings. And in each of those rings, she gave some different strength or powers. There was power to disappear in some ring, fire in some, water in some and every such ring had some power. In the end, she had put a magical sheet on her world so that no evil sorceress or any evil force could harm her world. She had put half of those magical rings in her palace's big and secret cellar and had given the left half of the rings to her son. While dying, she had made her son the king of this world and told her son to distribute these rings among the Amazindar's people wisely, according to their ability and capability," the man told this entire chronicle to me. "This is the real history of our World."

I was completely calm after listening to him. The whole chronicle was stunning as well as emotional. Marina was a good sorceress and kind queen, I imagined her character.

"Don't you want to listen what happened after the death of Marina?" that man asked. "It's not completed yet."

"After Marina died, Joseph seized the entire kingdom under his control and had put all of the rings with him and hadn't distribute even a single ring to anybody. He had hired his own officials and people and only given the magical rings to the people whom he had selected without seeing their ability and capability. He started running his own government and own laws and rules. Joseph's son and more coming generation had also done the same. They all were cruel and the coming generations were even crueler than Joseph. All of those kings one by one had only focused in their luxury and ease. They had distributed those magical rings to their people or to the one who were in their support. The kings kept the most powerful ring with them and distributed the rest over to their people even to those who were not capable of it. They had completely destroyed the Marina's World. We all had suffered from this for more than six centuries and then one day, your dad came into this World," he suddenly stopped after saying this.

"What happened next?" I asked him

It was getting extremely curious to know what happened after that. His each and every words were coming as if he knew the future and the past.

He then continued

"When your father came to this world, he was very happy and surprised to see the new world. When your father came to this world, I was about 60 years old and your father was only twenty seven at that time. My life is more than the life of an ordinary man because the ring I am wearing gives me more life but will not make me immortal. It will only help us to live just more than the ordinary people," he narrated. "Now I am 96."

I was not surprised to hear this because after seeing this world nothing seemed to be more astonishing at that time.

I wondered he said that the rings were only distributed to those who were king's people or who were hired by king.

"Then how is wearing one of those magical rings in his finger?" I wondered. "It seemed to be strange"

I then asked him about his magical ring and how he got it if the rings were only been given to the royal people.

"This ring is not mine, It's of my grandfather's grandfather; my ancestors!" he said.

This means that the ring received by the grandfather is also available to the member of the same family, without seeing if they are worth of it or not. "That's unfair!"

"Of course, it was!" he said.

"What do you mean by it was? Isn't this practice going on?" I asked him suspiciously.

"It is yet to be told to you"

He then continued from where he left

"Your father came to this world but the most surprising thing was that he knew our language and was able to understand us very well. Everyone here speaks Ancient German which is now rarely spoken anywhere. I had met your father like I have met you but the only difference was I didn't know English at that time, and I also used to speak in ancient German only. He was very keen to know more about our World and the possibility of life here. I then told him the entire history like I am telling you. I then told him the whole incident, which we all suffered for many centuries. He listened to me calmly, and then the incident that happened after I completed will blow your mind," he stopped.

"What happened next?" I asked in curiosity as I was desirous to know what happened next.

"Sure! I shall continue then," he replied.

"After knowing the bad condition of our world, he became angry and encouraged us to ask for our rights. He asked us to go to the king for our rights. We all didn't listen to him as it was not practical for us to do what he told. After that we had explained him that if we did this then what we are getting now will also stop. But your father did not agree and went out on his own to fight," told the man to me.

"Did he won the battle?" I asked him, assuring my dad won.

He told me that my dad won the battle very easily but I imagined how that is possible as he was a king with magical powers and my dad was just a human with no supernatural powers, I assumed.

"How he won the fight without any powers?" I asked him desirously.

"Well, nobody knows how he won the fight because nobody had seen him fighting with the king at that time," he replied. "Only your dad can tell this!"

I moved my head up and down but didn't trust him as it was difficult to believe whatever he said.

"What happened after then?" I asked him, assuming the possibility of what could happen.

He then continued saying that my dad had become the king of Amazindar after defeating the previous King.

"Your dad continues to be the King," the man said.

I was shocked after hearing him as I couldn't believe my dad as a King. My dad told me a lie of working at club but in reality he was the King of that magical world.

"Where's my dad?" I asked him vociferously. "I want to meet him right now.

"You can't!" he said angrily "He has been ill since few days and nobody is allowed to meet him."

I got very angry after hearing this from him and angrily said, "If he is your king, then I am his son."

I couldn't let my father go like this and nobody can take care of my dad better than me.

I then told him to just tell me the way through which I can go to my dad. I asked him to help me but he didn't help. He seemed to be scared of something at that time and was not even telling me.

Suddenly, Robert STOOD UP.

"I will tell you why he is saying like that," he said loudly, looking seriously into my eyes.

"It's because of Arkoma,"

Chapter-14
Determination to Win

I find it difficult to believe. I'm not sure. I'm not certain. I'm not sure whether he's telling the truth.

"Arkoma" REALLY?

Arkoma had been the King of Egypt in third century then how is it possible for a person to be alive for more than 15 centuries, I asked surprisingly.

"No! It's not that Arkoma which you are thinking of," he replied, keeping his eyebrows down for a second. "He is the King's minister and the most powerful person after the King."

"He will be the next King of this World," the man said.

Suddenly Robert came into the conversation.

"But according to the rules of our world, the King's son will be given the seat after the King, not the minister," Robert said suddenly, intercepted in between.

That man went silent for a second then started saying "NO–BUT–AA," faltered the man.

I then told them to forget about these things once and focus on letting me reach my dad at any cost. No matter how tough it would be.

Then suddenly Robert stood up and showed his support for me. He agreed to help me and promised me to take me to my father in every situation and if he had to give his life for this, he was ready to give it.

Robert and I was looking in each other's eye as the spirit of bravery lightened in us. That man was looking towards both of us.

"May you both succeed," the man blessed.

We both then left the house and Robert took me back to his house.

We started doing the planning on how to reach my dad and how to hoax the guards and security. Robert knew this World better than me as he was living in Amazindar for more than fifteen years. Robert kept on thinking a way to reach inside the place. He was continuously moving from one side to another side in the hall. I was also searching for an idea but I knew that I couldn't do anything because it was not my world.

Suddenly Robert moved him head up in a jolt. It seemed he got an idea. Robert then told me to sit on the chair because he will be going to explain the whole idea to me.

I sat on the chair and told him to tell me the idea that could really help us to reach inside the palace where I could find my dad. Robert seemed to be very sure of his idea.

Robert started explaining me the entire idea. I listened to his idea and agreed as he knew the world better than me and maybe his idea will help us to reaching my dad.

"Robert idea was to go inside the palace in the mid night at half past one."

"In our world, the effect of magical power slows down at mid night and hence the best time to enter the palace is at half past one at mid night," Robert propelled. "We can meet your dad at that time."

Robert idea seemed to be interesting and therefore, I accepted it. I hugged Robert tightly as he was helping me a lot. If he couldn't be there, then it would have become difficult for me to do this all on my own.

It was going to be night so we decided to succeed the plan the next day midnight.

"Robert, we should sleep now. We will do the preparation tomorrow in the morning," I said to him.

"OK, you may sleep on the couch and I will sleep on the ground here," he said graciously.

"Both of us were waiting for the next night and I was excited to meet to meet my dad, but the fear was more than the excitement."

Chapter-15
Let's Move On

The next morning when I woke up. I suddenly saw Robert putting something in his bag. I gave a voice to him but he didn't listen. I called him once again and then he looked back.

"Oh Marc, Come and have breakfast with me," Robert said, looking enthusiastic.

He was very happy in the morning. I thought maybe he forgot about the planning we had done in the night. I asked him about the plan which we will be going to execute at the midnight.
He suddenly replied, "OH YES! DON'T WORRY."

Robert was looking little bit strange but maybe it's his personality or habit. Robert then took me to the kitchen and shown me a bag in which he had put all the necessary items which was going to help us in reaching inside the Palace. Robert had done all the planning and explained the same to me. We were all set to move. "LET'S MOVE ON."

Then, we both ate the breakfast and after the breakfast, Robert took me again to that man house whom we had the previous day. I asked Robert why he took me here but he only said to wait and watch. In a while, that man came inside, holding a neck chain in his hand. That necklace was magical.

"Marc, just wear this chain as it will be going to protect you from the effect of magic and will lower the effect of any magical attack on you.

I thanked him for giving me the chain. He then blessed us for us success and then we went away from there and came back to Robert's house. Robert and I started planning about the activity which were going to execute at midnight. It was all going very well. Whole day we kept on talking about the plan and how we will go inside the palace that is surrounded and protected by guards.

"Guards will also be having the magical rings with them, so be careful there," Robert said very quietly, in a careful manner.

The whole day had passed and then it was the time to execute our plan and go according to it. We both took our packed bags and hang it. It was one in the midnight when we left Robert's house for the Palace. We both then started moving quietly and slowly towards the Palace where my dad was. We both hadn't gone from the road but from the forest way as we thought nobody can see us if we will go from the forest way. We then entered the forest way and started moving towards the way that take to the Palace. I was not knowing anything about the route but Robert seemed to know the way to go inside the Palace.

Then finally Robert and I reached outside the Palace. We had hidden ourselves in the bushes and I was seeing if anybody is roaming around or not. There was nobody around the gate. It seemed strange to not see any guard on the gate. I thought it as the carelessness of the guard and ignored because a lot of guards on the Earth are also very careless. I thought this as common issue and then started moving quickly toward the entrance gate of the palace as nobody was there. I was following Robert and we both were running on our toes, rarely producing sound from our shoes. We finally reached inside the Palace. I got very happy at that time, but was unhappy by the security of the palace. "They don't care for the security of their King," I said to myself. "We have entered inside the palace so easily and we faced no difficulty in the way."

I felt good after reaching inside the palace, but was not as happy as I should be. At that time, I didn't why know why I am not happy.

We were finally inside the Palace and were finding the way to go inside the Palace secretly. I asked him what to do next. He kept on seeing around but didn't find any way to get inside the palace without anybody inking. We were standing idle and I was in stress as we were not getting even a clue for the next step.

Suddenly, my eyes fell on a window that was hidden behind a bush and was slightly visible. I thought of going inside the palace through the window.

"See there is a window behind the bush!" I told Robert.

I moved towards the window and found that the window was not locked from inside. It was a good chance for both of us to go inside. I called Robert, in a whispering manner.

Everything was going very smoothly and that is why I started to have a little doubt. Neither the watchman nor any people, everything seemed strange. I looked around to see if anybody is following me or not but nobody was there when I saw. I then sighed with relief.

"Let's go! Walk in before anyone sees," shuddered Robert. "We should move quickly.

Then I quickly came inside through the window and Robert also did the same and came inside. I looked around. As soon as I reached inside, I saw that I am in a small room that was covered from all the side and only a single window was there in that room, from which I had come. There was nothing in that room and it was completely empty. Designs that was made on the walls were keep changing in every forty seconds. I'd never seen any view like this before. I'd seen computer desktop wallpaper changing in every thirty second but had never seen a wall design changing like this. And more surprising thing was that the wall design were not still and were moving. The magic seemed to be quite powerful.

Suddenly a noise of foots came from outside the room.

"What was that noise?" I squeaked as I glanced nervously from the hole below the door knob.

I did not see a single watchman all the way and suddenly I was terrified to see some guards marching together. I went silent for some time and waited for them to go. After they had gone, I sighed with relief. Now, I could move on to the next step.

I finally asked Robert to go outside and find my dad. Robert seemed to be annoyed by something but I didn't ask him. Before opening the door, I looked from hole near the doorknob to see if somebody is there outside or not. I saw nobody outside and then opened the door a little. I again looked around but nobody was there. I sighed with relief. I told Robert to come behind him because this time, I was finding a way to reach my dad's room. I didn't even know in which room my dad will be, but still my hope was pushing me up to continue the search. Robert asked me to go to the right side but I asked him to go left side. Our conversation got stuck at left or right. I told him to come with me but he didn't listen and went to the right side. I felt that someone would definitely see us on the right, so I went to the left. Robert did not listen to me anymore and he went to the right. I felt like fishy and it was not a good sign. Robert had behaved strangely ever since he came inside the palace.

Robert had gone to the right, but I realized that he might return when he will felt his mistake. I waited for Robert there only. I was seeing in the right for Robert to enter. After some time, Robert finally entered from the right. I got very happy to see Robert coming, but as soon he started moving towards me, some guards and a person with a crown

on his head also started coming towards me. They were behind the Robert and Robert was in front.
"Robert, Who are they?" I asked fearfully as Robert had gone alone but hadn't come back alone.

"They have come to meet you Marc," Robert replied. In an evil manner, slowly coming towards me. "They will regard you Mr. Marc Faladian."
I started stepping my steps back. I was frightened and was full of sweats. At that time, I didn't know what to do.

"They all were coming towards me with the intension of killing me."

Chapter-16
A Way to Escape

It seemed to be a disaster coming to me. I quickly looked back and started to run in order to escape. I ran so fast as if the swarm of bees were there behind me. They kept on chasing me. They started throwing magical spells on me but none of them touched me.

"Robert, you ditcher!" I blurted, while running in order to escape from them.

I used my whole strength in escaping. I kept on running from one place to another, finding a safe place to hide. They tried to stop me a lot but I didn't stop. I went to the basement and searched for a safe place to hide. I hid myself under a table. They were just on the first floor and I was in the basement.

Suddenly, my head got hit by the table under which I had hidden myself.

"What was that noise?" squeaked Robert as he heard some noise from the basement.

I was completely able to hear what they were talking. I was not too far from them. They were talking with each other about where I had gone.

"Arkoma, maybe he is hidden on the first floor," Robert gagged.

Robert had cheated me so hard that I could not believe he would do this to me. I started hating

Robert. Now I could understand why I had faced no problem in coming inside the palace. It was all planned and Robert is so clever that he didn't even let me get an ink of his plan. The more gullible he was becoming, the more devilish he was. I was stunned to Robert devil avatar as he had completely destroyed my trust on him. I got very angry and decided to find my dad at any cost.

"Neither Robert nor his flatterer can separate me from my dad. I will be definitely meet my dad," I determined angrily. "Nobody can stop me."

I got completely filled with energy. I decided to make my my own plan in order to reach my dad.

I then came out from under the table quietly. I couldn't go to my dad directly through stairs or from the hall as the guards were now more alert. I looked around to see if there is something that could help me. I didn't find any special equipments but found an old gate in the basement.

"A gate in the basement?" I asked myself suspiciously. "What can be the need of a gate in the basement?"

I then moved toward that gate to see what's there behind it. I tried to pull the gate but it didn't move even a millimeter. I then got more curious to know what's there behind the gate.

The gate was dusty, it seemed that nobody used to come in the basement often. I then blowed wind from my mouth to remove the dust, atleast a little bit. Suddenly while blowing the wind, I saw a hollow handprint made on the door. There was no doorknob or handle on the door, only a hand print was made on it.

That handprint didn't seemed to be of an ordinary person. It seemed to be of a big animal or a giant as the handprint was quite big.

I then looked at my hand and thought to put my hand on the handprint. I then slowly moved my hand toward that hand print and put my hands on it, keeping my eyes close. I opened my eyes and felt that nothing much has happened. Suddenly I felt that the handprint is now moving. I slowly turned the handprint clockwise and the brass core made a slight sound similar to a fingernail dragging on a countertop as the lock tailpiece dragged in its housing and engaged the deadbolt. As the deadbolt moved to the end of its travel, I heard a subdued ker-chunk sound as the deadbolt was automatically spring-assisted to the totally unlocked position. The gate was now unlocked!

I felt like if my hand is the key to open the lock. Maybe, it is, but at that time I was not sure.

The gate is unlocked and I got more curious to see what's there behind the gate.

Chapter-17
The Magical Ring and the Trickster

I opened the door and could not see anything beyond it because there was no light behind the door. I thought to move one step ahead the door but was confused where to put my first step, as I could only see darkness behind the door.

The moment I was looking behind the door, suddenly I saw a beam of light. I hadn't seen that light when I had opened the gate but suddenly it started appearing after some time. That light was coming towards me at a great speed. When I looked at it more closely, I saw that it was not a beam of light but a golden eagle which was coming towards me.

I got scared and tried to close the gate but it didn't work as the gate was jammed at one position was not moving.

"Oh my GOD! What should I do now?" I quavered.

That eagle came at a great speed and hit me. I fell down on my back as the eagle stroke me too hard.

For a second, my eyes got closed in a slight temporary pain when the eagle hit me. It had spread the golden glitters and suddenly got disappeared, leaving the ashes of golden glitter. It really seemed to be magical. That gate also get closed soon after the eagle disappeared.

Suddenly my eyes fell upon an envelope lying on the floor. That envelope was lying on the floor, just in front of the gate.

"From where did this envelope come from? There was nothing here some time ago," I wondered as it seemed to be strange.

Then I opened that envelope without thinking much and found a ring inside that letter. That ring was a magical ring as there was a very tine sculpture of a blue dragon on that ring. It was looking amazing. The base of the ring was golden in color, and something more was written on that ring that I couldn't understood.

I wondered if that ring can do powerful magic or not. I started wearing that ring slowly but suddenly Robert along with guards came inside the Basement. I quickly had put that ring in my upper suit pocket and they didn't get any doubt on me. They saw me in the basement and started laughing with evil smile.

"Now you cannot escape," Robert stated as they had entirely covered me from all sides.

I never thought Robert would be such a big trickster. They all had covered me from all the sides and there was no way to escape.

"I had never thought you will do this to me Robert," I said to Robert. "I trusted you but you…."

Robert ignored me and then ordered his guards to arrest me and put me in prison.

At that time, I didn't knew why he is doing that all with me.

"What did I do to you?" I asked him anxiously. "What do you want from me?"

"Ha!"

"You are the thorn in my path." Caterwauled Robert.

I did not understand all his things at that time. After all, how am I cutting his path? He was just looking at me angrily and was not even trying to understand my point.

"What do you mean by that?" I interrogated.

He kept looking me for some time.

"Oh Marc, you are so innocent. Do you remember what I told you about my family? I told you that I have no family. Sorry I lied to you! I have one." "I am the son of Arkoma, the minister of the king."

I was surprised to hear that. I was just stunned.

"So why did you do such a big drama with me?" I surprisingly asked.

"Because if our king cum your father came to know that you are here in this world, then he will give you the throne of his king in place of my father Arkoma and I will not let this happen," Robert spilled in anger, and didn't even notice that he spoke out all the truth in front of the guards also.

He then gave the order to his guards to arrest me. All the guards started coming towards me to arrest. One of the guards took his ring and put a magical spell on me using his ring. Perhaps that spell had the power to faint. I suddenly started feeling dizzy and in few seconds fell on the ground unconsciously.

When I opened my eyes, I found myself in prison. I suddenly started worrying, I was looking for a way out but could not find a way out of the prison. I started splashing and got extremely worried.

"Bastard Robert! I will definitely punish you for your bad deeds."

I started shaking the bars of the prison and tried opening it but it didn't work and was only a wastage of time.

The door was magical and was not even having a lock. It seemed to be locked by magic, and only magic could open it.

I was completely stuck there, and no way was visible at that time. Tears welled from deep inside and coursed down my cheeks. Tears spilled over and flowed down my face like a river escaping a dam. A solemn tear fell down my cheek; my body looked calm compared to how tangled my mind was. I began anathematizing myself for why I had come in this world.

"I left my home alone. My mom, sister and all the family members must be worrying," I realized and imagined their condition.

My whole face was filled with tears. My tears were falling on the ground too. Suddenly a single tear fell upon my upper suit pocket and straight away that ring that I had put in that pocket started glowing. My all attention went towards that ring.

I quickly took out that ring from my pocket and started looking at its brightness. For the next few minutes, I kept seeing that ring, holding in my hands.

"It's Amazing!" I exclaimed as the ring seemed to be brighter when I took it out from the pocket.

I moved my middle finger to put on the ring. I slowly started moving putting that ring into my middle finger. I was nervous and frightened at that time. But I gathered my confidence and inserted that ring in one fell swoop.

Nothing major happened in the next four to five seconds. But suddenly after few seconds, that ring started glowingly very brightly like that of sun. My eyes were half closed with creases on the forehead and some irritation in the muscles around the eyes. It was all because of the extreme brightness of the light that came from the right.

After a while, that light beamed and then got normal. The glow of the light got stopped. It was all normal with the ring.

I didn't feel any change in the body but was feeling quite more energetic and powerful than before. Suddenly then I felt like if energy is running around my body instead of blood. My body started producing some energy waves. I started feeling more powerful as if I had gotten some super heroes powers.

"Definitely the ring has given me this strength," I assumed as I was feeling energetic.

I didn't worry because I was knowing that the ring is magical and this ring is giving me all of these powers, but didn't know why this ring had chosen me only.

Immediately a beam of light came out from my body and busted all around.

I was stunned to see that all happenings. I was feeling more powerful than ever. I felt like as if my blood had been exchanged by energy cells. I then looked toward that ring, it seemed to be all normal with that ring even after the burst.

I then thought to get out of the prison using the ring but I didn't know how to use that ring at that time. I moved my finger and tried a lot of filmy spells but they all were waste and useless. I kept trying various methods, but nothing happened. Finally I got very angry because I tried a lot but nothing worked.

"What a bullshit ring this is! It's not working," I shouted angrily.

I then moved my hand and put it into the punch posture. I put my hands in the punch posture as I got very angry when none of the methods worked.

As I placed my hand in that position, on the spot a beam of ring suddenly came out and broke the magical door of the entire prison in which I was. The door totally melted entirely just after the exposure of beam of ring on it.

My body was filling with energy and I was feeling more powerful than ever. The GOD was helping me and nobody could stop me to meet my dad and take him back to the Earth.

I decided to take revenge from each of those people took me in danger and problems.

“Now I had power.”

“Now the time had come to take his father back home.”

Chapter-18
Goodbye to the World

Now the ring was the only thing that could help take my dad back home. I came out of the prison and started moving toward the great hall. I was no more in fear from the guards and Robert.

I then came to the Great Hall, and the Robert along with his trickster dad Arkoma was also there. We both looked at each other, but suddenly he tried to throw a magical spell on me but my ring saved me from that spell.

I moved my right hand in which I was wearing the ring and moved it toward Robert. A beam came out of the ring and injured Robert. My ring seemed to be extremely powerful. Arkoma kept on seeing me like as he saw a magical ring in my hand also.
"Marina's ring! How did you get that?" He asked shockingly, in a surprising manner.

"I didn't find this ring but this ring found me," I replied, showing that ring to him.
I used my ring spell and wrecked the entire great hall. I was very angry with me.

Suddenly, Arkoma tried to confuse me using a confusing magical spell but it didn't work because my ring saved me from that attack as well. I didn't know how that ring is saving me from each and every attack. That ring was not like any other magical ring.

Every attack on me was going in waste, and I felt more confidence on my power then. None of the guards dare to attack. I again point my ring toward Arkoma.

"Tell me where my father is otherwise…." I blurted, as I was going to do another attack on him if he will not answer.

"Wait-Wait! I will tell you everything," Arkoma vacillated as he got scared after I point out my magical ring on him with the intension to attack. "Even before you came, your father was running very sick and so he has put himself to rest in the building behind the palace. You can go and meet him there," he answered, gasping in fear at the sight of him.

I then desperately ran to meet my dad. I woke up with tears of joy towards the back building of my palace. I went inside the building behind the palace and stood outside a big royal door—"he must be here."

It was all very exciting as I will be going to meet my dad after facing so many problems.

"My mom and all the family members will get happy to see my dad," I imagined their happiness.

I then gently pushed the door from my right hand.

"The door slowly started moving inwards, it was opening. My heart was beating faster than usual. That moment was the happiest moment for me and the curiosity was decorating it.

As soon as the door was opened my eyes fell on the bed. I finally saw my dad. That moment was like if my all my desires are fulfilled. I felt as if I had met the almighty. I felt like if an orphan got his parents. I felt like if a poor got a billion dollar, but it was more than that for me. The words are not enough to describe my feeling when I saw my dad after going through so much difficulties.

I then started moving slowly towards my dad. I didn't know how to behave at that time. My body was shivering as I was happier than ever.

My dad was sleeping, looking quite tired. I sat behind beside him. I started weeping as I couldn't control my emotions.

Suddenly, my dad woke up!

"It's you son?"

"Yes dad, it's me" I told him with a smile on face with tears.

My dad quickly hugged me and me too. Tears started coming out from my dad's eyes, but it was the tears of happiness. This moment was as much a nostalgic one as it was enjoyable.

That feeling and moment cannot be elaborate in some few words. A son to meet his father who was declared killed by his own family.

"I knew you are alive," I said.

"I knew that one day you will definitely find this world," my dad said, proudly looking into my eyes after a long time.

"How did you get the ring of Marina in your hand? It means that you are the one whom Marina has chosen," dad stuttered.

I didn't understand what he was saying but I didn't even ask him about that. I then quickly told him to leave this world and come back to Earth but he refused to leave. He told me that if he leaves Amazindar then what will happen to his people, who will take care of them?

Dad words were also worth noting.

Suddenly, Arkoma and Robert came running inside the room. They get stopped after seeing me sitting beside my dad; their king. They both went numb and didn't say a single word in front of the king, but I told my dad everything about Robert and his father Arkoma who was planning a conspiracy to become king. I told my father what all those tricksters, Robert and Arkoma did to me when I came to Amazindar.

My dad stood up and ordered the guards to put both of them in the prison for their entire life.

"I trust you Arkoma but you broke it," My dad enraged as it was a betrayal. "Take their rings back from them."

After that, both of them start apologizing but my dad did not forgive them and imprisoned both of them for their entire life.

It was all good after then.

Since then, my father and I left that world forever and freed the world from king's governance and allowed everyone to live their lives happily and freely.

Answers of Some Questions

What happened in Amazindar after Marc and his dad left?

After they left, a man of the Amazindar won the trust of his people on his ability and strength, and then he ruled as a good king without any discrimination.

What was the secret behind the letter written in ancient German?

That letter was actually sent by Marc's father to Marc from Amazindar.

What was written in that secret letter?

In that letter, Mark's father wrote that after he dies, his entire legacy will be of Marc.

Did Marc's mother already know anything about Amazindar from before?

Yes, Marc's mother knew all this, but not from the beginning, but she also came to know when she and Marc's dad met for the last time, before his father left for the Amazindar.

Why didn't she tell Marc anything about that magical world and the secret behind his dad's sudden disappearance?

She was very scared and did not want Marc's life to be like his dad and she didn't want her son to go in that world and rule only.

What happened to the Marina's magical ring after they left?

Marc brought the Marina's magical ring with himself only to the Earth and kept it safe.

Through which door did they return to their world?

The answer will be very surprising because one door was in the store room of their own house which was hidden. The same door was often used by Marc's father to go and come from Amazindar

About the Author

Nikhil Sharda was born in 2005 in New Delhi, India. Growing up, he was fascinated with computer, and this interest led to the earlier exposure to digital world since he was drawn to activities such as coding, editing, writing and much more.

Along with these talents, he's been a state finalist competitive at Scratch (visual programming language) at the age of 10. His love toward the computer and the digital gadgets and software is insane. Nikhil considers his faith and family to be most important to him. He is currently an Indian student, pursuing his high school along with writing books.

In Walking into the Mystery, it narrates the fictional tale of a boy who had gone on a journey to solve a mystery behind his dad's sudden disappearance but later on discovered a lot of unbelievable things and one of those includes a magical world.